The Swing of the Sea

Molly Hagan

A SAMUEL FRENCH ACTING EDITION

SAMUEL FRENCH

FOUNDED 1830

SAMUELFRENCH.COM

ISBN 978-0-573-70195-5

www.SamuelFrench.com
www.SamuelFrench-London.co.uk

FOR PRODUCTION ENQUIRIES

UNITED STATES AND CANADA
Info@SamuelFrench.com
1-866-598-8449

UNITED KINGDOM AND EUROPE
Plays@SamuelFrench-London.co.uk
020-7255-4302

Each title is subject to availability from Samuel French, depending upon country of performance. Please be aware that *THE SWING OF THE SEA* may not be licensed by Samuel French in your territory. Professional and amateur producers should contact the nearest Samuel French office or licensing partner to verify availability.

MUSIC USE NOTE

Licensees are solely responsible for obtaining formal written permission from copyright owners to use copyrighted music in the performance of this play and are strongly cautioned to do so. If no such permission is obtained by the licensee, then the licensee must use only original music that the licensee owns and controls. Licensees are solely responsible and liable for all music clearances and shall indemnify the copyright owners of the play(s) and their licensing agent, Samuel French, against any costs, expenses, losses and liabilities arising from the use of music by licensees. Please contact the appropriate music licensing authority in your territory for the rights to any incidental music.

IMPORTANT BILLING AND CREDIT REQUIREMENTS

If you have obtained performance rights to this title, please refer to your licensing agreement for important billing and credit requirements.

THE SWING OF THE SEA was first produced at Arcadia University in Glenside, PA on December 1, 2011. The performance was directed by Mark Wade, with sets by Michael Kerns costumes by Alisa Sickora Kleckner, sound by Daniel Perelstein, and lighting by Joshua Schulman. The Production Stage Manager was Jamie Lee Dagen. The cast was as follows:

BOOTS . . . . .Rachel Diamond

EGGS . . . . Alex Pappaterra

PETER . . . . .Trevor Fayle

Also featuring: Nicole Samuel, Dawnelle Jewell, and Jackie Sherman

CHARACTERS

BOOTS – A thirteen year old girl who wears yellow rain boots even when it's not raining.

PETER – An almost thirteen year old boy.

EGGS – A twelve year old boy.

SETTING

The set should be fluid and need only suggest the following locations:

A tree house
A closet
An imagined beach
A school hallway with lockers
An imagined school cafeteria
A gymnasium

AUTHOR'S NOTES

A Note on the Characters: While Boots, Eggs and Peter are adolescents they may be played by actors of any age so long as there is uniformity within the cast. That being said, older actors should not "play young" or in any way portray the characters as caricatures of children in speech, dress or demeanor.

Regarding Peter: It is especially important that Peter be played as a living, breathing boy and not a ghost, apparition or figment of the imagination.

A Note on Tone: It is important to play each scene in the moment (particularly the last scene) so as to not let the melancholy of Peter's death pervade the play. No moping.

The method and/or circumstances of Peter's suicide should never be addressed or implied in the design or anywhere else in the production.

A Note on the Set: It is my intention that this play can be performed on the cheap. Leaves can be bits of paper, the tree house can be a simple platform, etc. Theatricality! Imagination!

I have desired to go
Where springs not fail,
To fields where flies no sharp and sided hail
And a few lilies blow.

And I have asked to be
Where no storms come,
Where the green swell is in the havens dumb,
And out of the swing of the sea.

– Gerard Manley Hopkins

*For Ryan, whose patience and skill were instrumental
in the shaping of this play*

One

(A tree house, old and crumbling.

It smells like moss.

Outside it is raining.

Inside the tree house a bowl catches raindrops falling through a hole in the roof.

A flashlight sits in the corner.

BOOTS *alone, wearing yellow rain boots.*

She blows kisses into the air to an unseen crowd of farewellers.)

BOOTS. A kiss!
For you.
And you and you
and you.
Au revoir!
Au revoir and *bon voyage.*

*(***EGGS*** *enters up the rope ladder wearing one book bag and holding another.*

He and the bags are wet from the rain.)

EGGS. I have your bag.
What are you doing?

*(***BOOTS*** *walks.*

She blows a kiss out the window.)

We're going to be late.

*(***BOOTS*** *doesn't answer.)*

Did you do the worksheet? The math one?
It was pretty easy, actually.
Fractions.

It didn't take me very long.

You can copy if you want.

(beat)

I guess it wouldn't be a big deal or anything
if you didn't do it I mean.

I'm sure Mr. Fleming won't even care.

He probably won't even notice.

That class is so dumb, right?

(beat)

Do you think he'll say something?

Maybe he won't even mention it.

But that would be weird.

But I mean, what would he be like,
sorry? Or something.

I don't even know.

What are you doing in the tree house?

You missed the bus.

You left your book bag at the bottom of your driveway.

In the rain.

What's going on?

Boots.

I followed you

Did you see me?

BOOTS. I'm bidding farewell.

EGGS. That's not very funny.

BOOTS. What if we were on a ship and we were leaving the
dock?

Wouldn't that be the craziest thing?

If I had a handkerchief I would wave one. Do you think
people still have handkerchiefs?

I wonder where you can even get one anymore. That's
so sad, you know what I mean?

EGGS. I watched you.

I saw you leave your book bag in the rain.

I got it for you.

Will you just take it so we can go?

We're going to miss the thing at the flagpole.

BOOTS. Megan bought her prom dress on Saturday.

She tried it on but she wouldn't let me touch it.

This is what she looks like when she walks in her heels.

Heel, toe. Heel, toe.

Do you think they have handkerchiefs where they sell prom dresses?

EGGS. I can't go without you.

BOOTS. I bet they do.

But I bet it's not the same.

EGGS. Did you even know that they're doing some kind of ceremony this morning?

For Peter. Before the bell?

Around the flagpole, we're supposed to stand around the flagpole and

hold hands or something.

I can't do that. The whole thing creeps me out.

Do you even realize?

Everything is different now.

You have to come with me.

I can't hold somebody else's hand.

BOOTS. Remind me to tell you this thing about leaves.

EGGS. Boots!

BOOTS. What?

EGGS. What's wrong with you?

BOOTS. *Wrong* with me?

EGGS. It's like you don't even know how to act –

BOOTS. I don't know how to *act?*

EGGS. I'm sorry, but –

BOOTS. How old are you, Eggs?

(*They've been through this before.*)

EGGS. Twelve, but I'm almost –

BOOTS. And how old am I?

EGGS. Thirteen.

BOOTS. Just checking.

    What were you saying?

EGGS. I'm sorry, okay?

    But I was just saying.

    I was saying how this whole thing is weird for me,

    maybe it's not for you

    but it looks like,

    it's like

    you don't even know how to act

    when real life scary things happen.

    (beat)

BOOTS. *(matter-of-fact)* What I was going to say,

    about the leaves,

    is that it's funny how small they are but the piles get so big.

    That's all I was going to say.

EGGS. You're being a real jerk.

    I'm leaving now.

BOOTS. The lady next door was walking her dog today.

EGGS. Boots, seriously.

    It isn't funny.

    I want to go now.

BOOTS. Why did you come here then?

EGGS. I don't know –

BOOTS. Do you want to go to the flagpole or whatever?

    Or do you want to be with me?

    *(**EGGS** doesn't respond.)*

    The lady next door.

    She was walking her dog this morning when I was waiting for the bus.

    She was walking really slow

    and I could see her face really clearly.

And without even thinking about it or anything,
I said, "Hi," as she passed.
I didn't even realize I had said it until after she was
gone.
And I couldn't help it
but I started thinking, like,
what if she died today?
What would I remember about her in this exact
moment?
And I tried to memorize all those things.
And then I thought, that's the problem.
That I didn't do that
with him.

EGGS. No one knew.

No one expected.

(long beat)

How do you think he did it?

BOOTS. What?

EGGS. How do you think he *did* it?

Did they tell you?

BOOTS. Tell me what?

(pause)

Oh.

(quietly) I don't know.

(long pause)

EGGS. You don't

I mean

Did you think about it?

BOOTS. *No.*

EGGS. I mean not even like

BOOTS. I don't want to talk about it.

EGGS. I thought about what would happen if my mom died
once.

EGGS. *(cont.)* And I thought about
the couch being empty.

Or where she sits at the kitchen table.

Or it being quiet
in the hall
when she paces between my room and hers before
school.

BOOTS. Eggs.

EGGS. Yeah?

BOOTS. You're embarrassing me.

EGGS. I keep thinking about the last time we saw him?
Leaving school?

We all walked out of the door by the gym.

Do you remember the last thing he said to us?

He was like, "See you guys." Like he was saying good-
bye to *us*, specifically.

Does that, like connect the three of us for all time or
is that stupid?

BOOTS. Shut up.

EGGS. But now we'll remember it forever, you know what
I mean?

BOOTS. No.

EGGS. Why?

BOOTS. Because that's not the last thing he said to me.

EGGS. But it was.

He was walking the other way, remember?

He said it and turned around and we started walking
home.

Me and you.

BOOTS. No.

EGGS. Yes.

BOOTS. That wasn't the last time I saw him.

EGGS. What?

BOOTS. That wasn't the last time I saw him.

I saw him after that.

EGGS. Where?

BOOTS. At the tree house.

EGGS. When? I mean –

that night?

That's impossible.

Because you said

you said you were going to your aunt's house for dinner.

You

BOOTS. We didn't end up going.

EGGS. So you went to the tree house?

BOOTS. I had told him to meet me there,

I told him at his locker after school.

Before we saw you.

EGGS. And – what?

You had a party or something?

BOOTS. He showed up so late that I thought he wasn't even coming.

EGGS. And?

BOOTS. It was dark. Like really dark.

Without a flashlight, I couldn't see anything at all.

It was weird – I don't even remember any stars.

EGGS. Okay. So it was dark.

BOOTS. It was boring.

EGGS. Boring.

Boring like – ?

BOOTS. Boring like, whatever.

Like you didn't miss anything if that's what you –

EGGS. So what was it?

BOOTS. What was what?

EGGS. What was the last thing he said to you?

(*pause*)

BOOTS. I –

I don't remember.

(*A leaf falls from the hole in the ceiling.*

BOOTS *picks it up.*)

Where did this come from?

EGGS. Where did what come from?

I don't understand.

If you had this secret meeting.

If it was special or whatever.

How can you not remember?

How can you not remember the last thing he said?

BOOTS. It wasn't a secret meeting.

I barely remember any of it at all.

EGGS. It was only a few *days* ago.

BOOTS. I *know.*

EGGS. I don't believe you.

BOOTS. What do you mean you don't believe me?

EGGS. I think you're lying about the whole thing.

About forgetting.

You know.

You just don't want to say it.

BOOTS. I'm not lying.

EGGS. Then tell me what happened.

BOOTS. I don't know.

(*Beat.*

She thinks.)

BOOTS. I remember he came up the rope ladder – finally.

And he was all out of breath, and he's like,

Sorry. And he goes, All the way here I was trying to think of something like –

And he tells me all these things about dropping his watch in the toilet or whatever, but then he said how lame they all sounded.

(pause)

And then

and he asked me where my rain boots were.

Because I wasn't wearing them.

And I told him that I was giving them a rest.

To do something different.

And then I asked him

I asked him

If he brought his flashlight

EGGS. And then what?

BOOTS. And then

And then I don't remember

(A leaf falls.)

EGGS. You must remember something.

What did you guys – do?

BOOTS. I – we

We listened for owls.

I remember that.

EGGS. And then what?

BOOTS. We told stories.

EGGS. Stories?

BOOTS. I think so.

EGGS. What kind of stories were they?

BOOTS. I –

I can't remember.

(A leaf falls.)

EGGS. Were they happy stories or sad ones?

BOOTS. I don't know.

(A leaf falls.)

(A breeze.)

EGGS. Were they ghost stories? Were they about people we
  know?

BOOTS. I'm not sure.

> *(More leaves are falling.)*

Look at the leaves.

EGGS. What?

BOOTS. Look at all the leaves.

EGGS. What leaves?

  What are you talking about?

  You really expect me to believe

  that you can't remember a single thing that happened?

  I mean –

  what did he say?

  Did he say anything about me?

> *(**BOOTS** shakes her head and shrugs.*
>
> *A few leaves fall.*
>
> *A gust of wind.)*

EGGS. I mean –

  this is kind of a big deal.

BOOTS. I just can't remember anything else.

EGGS. What was the last thing he said to you?

  You really can't remember the last thing he said?

  Not even that?

> *(A few leaves fall.)*

BOOTS. No.

> *(beat)*

No.

> *(A few leaves fall.*
>
> ***BOOTS** picks them up and examines them in her hand.*
>
> *More leaves fall.*
>
> *The sound of wind.)*

EGGS. Boots –

did you hear me?

(More leaves fall.

The sound of wind.)

Boots?

(A wall of leaves.)

Boots.

(When they settle **EGGS** *is gone.*

BOOTS *emerges.*

The sound of wind is gone.

The light is dimming.

Stillness.

BOOTS *looks around.*

She looks out the window, after **EGGS**.

She doesn't see him.

The flashlight is still there.

She picks it up and turns it on.

The light falls on the bowl.

The dripping which occurred during the entire previous scene has stopped.

She waits for it to resume.

She shines her light at the hole in the roof above the bowl.

Nothing.

She shines her light into the bowl.

Strange.

She picks it up. She turns it over.

It's empty.

She replaces the bowl and backs away.

She calls out in the direction of the rope ladder.)

BOOTS. Eggs. Are you still there?

You can come up if you're still there.

(Long silence.

And then, finally:

The water drips into the bowl again.

She breathes a sigh of relief and, relaxing again, steps onto the pile of leaves with the flashlight in her hand.

But rather than coming to a stop on the pile, she falls through.

And continues to fall.

The light from **BOOTS***'s flashlight swirls to the floor.*

She stands with the flashlight beneath her chin.

Only her face is lit.

The sound of waves.

She looks around.)

Hello?

(Ragtime music plays from far away.

She spots a figure in the distance.

And calls out:)

Eggs?

(A bright light.

Flurry.

Dark.)

Two

(EGGS sits pretzeled on the floor,

hiding in the recesses of his closet.

He is surrounded by piles of dirty clothes.)

EGGS. My closet.

(He runs his fingers over the clothes.)

My clothes.

When I get scared I like to come in here and I take my hamper and tip it over

and I wrap myself in dirty clothes.

Which is gross, I guess.

If I hold myself like this for long enough the things around me start to fade in and out and become the same thing,

like a holographic baseball card when you tip it back and forth.

(Touching an article.)

A broken pair of headphones, which I would be listening to if I hadn't sat on them.

(An article.)

My baseball jersey from last Saturday's game. Which we lost.

(An article.)

My tennis shoes, with the laces all knotted together.

(He throws them down.)

I went to school today without you.

Your desk is still there in case you were wondering. It's empty though, obviously.

Are you going to the Favorites Dance on Friday?

I thought we could go together so it wouldn't be awkward.

EGGS. *(cont.)* We can headbang near the bleachers. That would be pretty cool.

(beat)

Should I ask Boots to the dance or would that be weird? It would be weird.

When we were kids, she saw me naked.

I mean, I don't remember or anything, but what if she does?

What if I asked her and all of a sudden, the memory came rushing back – I would die.

Or.

Sorry. I didn't mean that.

Was I a bad friend?

(beat)

Boots didn't come to school today at all. I thought she would.

If you were here, here's what you would say:

Be *FUNNIER.* Girls will like you.

If you were here, here's what I would say:

I'm *TRYING!*

(He laughs.

He catches himself.)

That wasn't very funny.

Three

(In the dark.)

BOOTS. Hello?

> *(She swings the flashlight around: nothing.)*
> Eggs?
> Is somebody there?
> *Hello?*
> *(Fast footsteps in the sand.*
> *Breathing.*
> *She swings the light around.*
> **PETER**'s *face.*
> *He's smiling.*
> *He's out of breath from running.*
> *But he's blurry in the dark.)*

BOOTS. Peter?

PETER. Boots!

BOOTS. What are you doing here?

> *(pause)*

PETER. Are you shaking?

BOOTS. No.

PETER. Your light is shaking.
Are you afraid?

BOOTS. No.
I just don't like the dark.

PETER. Oh, I'm sorry.

> *(**PETER** pulls out a flashlight.*
> *He turns it on.*
> *Each shines a light on the other's face.*
> *Their figures appear dimly.)*

*(We see **PETER** more clearly.*

He is not a ghost.

He is not ghostlike.

He is a 13-year-old boy.)

PETER. *(cont.)* Is that better?

BOOTS. What is this place?

PETER. You can't tell?
This is the beach.

(The sound of waves.)

When I heard your voice I came running but my feet
kept sinking in the sand.
And the whole way
I was thinking of something funny to tell you like,
I flushed my watch down the toilet!
or
I thought you said *ten* thirty!
or
Time flies! Or something.
But then I realized none of it was that funny.
(Beat.

BOOTS *looks at him strangely.)*

What?

BOOTS. Nothing, it's just that
I've heard that before.
You said that exact same thing.

PETER. When?

BOOTS. That night.

PETER. What night?

BOOTS. The last night I saw you.

PETER. Oh, *that* night.

BOOTS. It's weird because that's basically one of the only
things I remember.

PETER. That's too bad.

BOOTS. I know.

PETER. No, I mean, that's really too bad.

Pretty much tragic.

BOOTS. Why?

PETER. I don't know. It's hard to really describe.

But the whole night – it was just –

there was a certain feeling.

BOOTS. Like – a happy feeling?

PETER. More than that. Like –

A celebration. Like a foghorn and streamers hanging
from the bow of a giant ship as it leaves a port.

Just like that kind of feeling.

Only we were in the tree house.

BOOTS. Wow.

PETER. Yeah.

Hey, no boots.

BOOTS. What?

PETER. *(pointing to her feet)* You're not wearing your rain
boots –

BOOTS. But I am wearing my rain boots –

PETER. I thought you were the kind of girl –

BOOTS. The kind of girl who always wears rain boots.

Even when it's not raining.

You said that too.

And then we listened for owls.

PETER. Owls?

BOOTS. Yeah, we listened for owls.

PETER. No, we didn't.

BOOTS. Of course we did. Why would I remember it if it
didn't happen?

PETER. I don't know. But I can tell you. That didn't happen.

BOOTS. Then what did we do?

What did we do after you said the thing about my
boots?

PETER. We started dancing.

    (**BOOTS** *laughs but sees that* **PETER** *is serious.*)

BOOTS. That's crazy. We were not dancing.

PETER. We were. You told me about Megan's prom dress.
    And we talked about prom.
    And then
    we started dancing.

BOOTS. Maybe we were talking about dancing.

PETER. No. We were dancing. And we talked about what it
    would be like when we go to prom.
    I said that you would wear a crown made out of leaves.
    And that I would fill my pockets with popsicle sticks
    and scatter them on the floor where you walk.

BOOTS. Oh.

    (*beat*)

PETER. What?

BOOTS. Well, that's impossible.
    I just realized, there won't be any prom.

PETER. There won't be any prom?

BOOTS. No.

    (*Beat.*

    PETER *is disappointed.*)

PETER. Oh.

    (**BOOTS** *tries to bring him back.*)

BOOTS. Because
    Because maybe we were pretending we were old.

PETER. Old?

BOOTS. Yeah.

PETER. How old?

BOOTS. I don't know. Probably.
    One hundred years old.

PETER. I like that.

But.

You can't dance if you're one hundred.

BOOTS. Of course you can!

Let's dance like we're one hundred.

I'll show you how. You dance like this.

(She dances like she's one hundred.)

PETER. No. More like this.

(He dances like he's one hundred.

They laugh.

Beat.)

BOOTS. Here's how it happens:

We are both one hundred.

But we are young and strong

and we run away from the old folks home.

You tie a rope of bed sheets and Twister mats together
and throw it out the window of your bedroom.

You used to be a pilot in the Navy and you know how
to scale down walls.

Because they teach you that kind of thing.

Anyway, when you reach the ground, you throw rocks
at my window on the second floor.

And I open my window

and I just –

jump, like this.

(She jumps in the air.)

PETER. And it's not very far and I catch you

in the Twister mat.

Because I used to be a firefighter and I've had to catch
a lot of people,

jumping out of windows.

BOOTS. What did I used to be?

PETER. You did a lot of things.

    You're a hundred years old.

    You've done everything.

    But.

    Your favorite things were –

    you were a great artist.

    You painted giant murals, as big as a city.

    Forests and Beaches.

    Long, long hallways.

    So big and so real

    that people tried to walk right into them.

BOOTS. And after that I was the captain of a great ship, or no.

    I built a raft out of a redwood tree

    and sailed around the world.

    No one's done *that.*

PETER. But *you* did. Because you're different than other people.

BOOTS. I'm like you.

PETER. You're just like me.

    (beat)

    So

    I catch you.

    And we run away together.

    We run to the beach because you have your raft

    built out of a redwood tree waiting for us there.

BOOTS. Do we get tired from running?

PETER. We never get tired.

    We don't grow old the way other people grow old.

    We're still the same as we've always been.

    So, we run and we get to the beach.

BOOTS. And it's a night without stars, like this one.

PETER. There's not one single star in the sky.

    You can't even see the moon.

That's how they don't find us.

Everyone and our families.

Because they've been chasing us the whole way.

BOOTS. The only light comes from their flashlights.

(She swings her flashlight around.

Her light reflects off the ocean.)

And it reflects off the ocean, but they never find us.

PETER. They never find us.

And we stand on the beach and we look at the empty sky.

And it looks like one of your murals.

And then I say,

to the lady in the crown,

"May I have this dance?"

And you say –

BOOTS. I'm too shy.

PETER. But then we compromise.

And we dance like we're one hundred and at the prom at the same time.

BOOTS. Because we have all the time in the world.

PETER. Because we have all the time in the world.

(beat)

BOOTS. How long will it be like this?

PETER. I don't know.

(beat)

BOOTS. Do you think –

even if we stayed here for a hundred years

that we would ever be as happy as we were that night?

PETER. What do you mean?

BOOTS. I mean

You said there was a certain feeling, like

foghorns and streamers.

I can't imagine ever being so happy.

PETER. Aren't you happy now?

BOOTS. Of course.

> *(beat)*

If we're dancing then where's the music?

PETER. We don't need music.

BOOTS. But.

If there were music, it would be Billie Holiday.
The slow one, that song I like, do you know it?

PETER. No. But I know Michael Jackson.
What about Billie Jean?

BOOTS. No, no.
It has to be Billie Holiday.
I'll teach it to you. If I can remember the words.

> *(She tries to remember the words.)*

Something about something familiar.
And then…

PETER. Is it happy or sad?

BOOTS. It's, well,
she's singing it to someone she loves.
It's a love song.
Anyways, she says she walks around
seeing the things she sees every day,
but everything,
even when she looks up at the moon,
all she can see is you.
Whoever she's singing it to, I mean.
I just like the song a lot.
You probably think that's weird.

PETER. That's not weird at all.
If I knew it, I bet I would like it too.

BOOTS. You really would.
I like it because it makes me think of
high heels with laces and a lot of buttons and ragtime,
even though it isn't ragtime.

And
and the blues.
And the moon.
And being happy and sad at the same time.
It's hard to explain.

PETER. I know exactly what you mean.

BOOTS. You do?

PETER. Yes.

How about this?
How about we dance to Billie Holiday.
We'll both close our eyes and
you sing the song in your head and I'll hear it.

BOOTS. Okay.

(They close their eyes.

BOOTS *sings the song in her head and* **PETER** *listens.*

They dance silently without touching.)

What happens next?

PETER. While we're dancing, I lean over and I whisper in
your ear.
I whisper, "O.K.K.B.W.P."

BOOTS. What does that mean?

PETER. And then we flicker our flashlights –

BOOTS. – But what does that mean? O.K.K.B.W.P.?

PETER. We flicker our flashlights at the sky.
And then,
we disappear.

*(***PETER** *drops his flashlight.)*

BOOTS. But what about the prom and the raft?
The Twister mat?
What happens to all of that?

PETER. They disappear too.

(The sound of waves.)

BOOTS. What did you say?

What about everyone? And our families?

(The sound of waves.)

PETER. I said we leave them behind.

(The sound of waves.)

BOOTS. *(louder, above the waves)* But why?

Wait! Peter!

*(**BOOTS** swings her flashlight around, but **PETER** is gone.*

The sound of waves.)

Four

(**BOOTS** *walks down the hallway at school.*

She stands at her locker.

EGGS *stands next to her at his locker.*

He opens his locker door.

He slams it shut.

BOOTS *doesn't look over.*

He opens his locker door.

He slams it shut.

BOOTS *doesn't look over.*

He does this a few times, finally:)

BOOTS. That's really annoying, actually.

EGGS. Oh, hey Boots. I didn't see you there.
My locker door. It's stuck.

(**BOOTS** *starts to walk away.*

She thinks of something.

She turns around quickly as **EGGS** *begins to speak.*

They speak at the same time.)

| **BOOTS.** Hey, I have a question for you. | **EGGS.** So, we missed you at the flagpole yesterday. |

(beat)

EGGS. And school. I guess you didn't come.
I called your house when I got home but your mom said
you were in the bathtub and wouldn't come out.

(embarrassed beat)

But um.
What were you going to say?

BOOTS. Oh.

EGGS. No, what?

BOOTS. Oh. Just
    have you ever heard of – O.K.K.B.W.P.?

EGGS. What?

BOOTS. The letters O.K.K.B.W.P.
    Have you heard that before?

(**EGGS** *thinks for several beats.*

Finally:)

EGGS. No.

BOOTS. Okay never mind.
    I'll see you later.

EGGS. Why?

BOOTS. It was just something I heard somewhere.

(*She begins to walk away.*)

EGGS. Wait!
    Just a sec,
    there are two things that I was supposed to tell you.

BOOTS. Yeah?

EGGS. I don't remember.

BOOTS. Okay. I'll see you later!

EGGS. Oh. I remember. One was,
    what I was going to say,
    was that
    Peter's mom called my mom this morning.

BOOTS. Oh.

EGGS. I just felt weird, you know.
    Saying it right out.
    But uh, she was saying
    I don't know if you know, but it was
    supposed to be Peter's –

BOOTS. I know.

EGGS. birthday, yeah. Tomorrow.
    Anyway, she wanted to see if,
    she wants to take a group of us,

of Peter's friends out. I think. For ice cream or
something.

(beat)

BOOTS. Yeah?

EGGS. Anyway, I just wanted to
     I was supposed to tell you
     that.

(beat)

BOOTS. Whatever, Eggs.

EGGS. What?

BOOTS. Whatever. I know you guys were really close. I get
     it.
     You don't have to keep rubbing it in my face every five
     seconds.

EGGS. What are you talking about?

BOOTS. I knew him too. You don't have to keep
     inviting me to things like I don't even know
     like I don't know what's going on
     like you know better.

EGGS. I'm not –

BOOTS. I knew him. We were friends. We were all friends.
     But me and him
     we were the same age.

(beat)

     We would have been the same age.

EGGS. I'm sorry.
     I didn't think you'd freak out.
     I just thought you should know.

BOOTS. I'm not *freaking out.*

EGGS. Okay.
     Okay.

     I just thought you should know.

BOOTS. I'm not freaking out.

EGGS. I know.

Okay.

BOOTS. I'm not *freaking out.*

EGGS. I know.

BOOTS. You said I didn't even know how to act.

EGGS. I didn't mean that.

BOOTS. You said it, but you know

I don't think you understand

anything.

EGGS. Boots.

I don't know what you're mad at me for.

BOOTS. I'm not *mad* –

EGGS. I'm not the one who died.

I'm –

BOOTS. Well, maybe it should have been.

(Silence.

The sound of waves.)

EGGS. I'm still here.

(Long pause.)

BOOTS. Eggs, I.

*(**BOOTS** reaches over and shuts his locker.)*

I fixed it.

EGGS. Yeah.

BOOTS. I have to,

I have to be,

what was the other thing you were going to tell me?

EGGS. I don't remember.

I'll see you.

*(**EGGS** walks away down the long hallway.*

BOOTS *rests her head on her locker.*

The sound of waves.

The sound of wind.

She looks up.

EGGS *is gone and the lockers open up*

one by one down the hall.

Water spills out like the ocean, covering the floor.

The sound of ragtime music far away.

BOOTS *looks around to make sure no one is watching.*

She opens her locker.

She takes out the flashlight.

She turns it on and wades into the sea.)

Five

(**BOOTS** *in the dark with her flashlight.*

She swings her flashlight around: nothing.

Then footsteps in the sand.

PETER *appears with his flashlight.*

They look at each other for a moment.)

BOOTS. What does O.K.K.B.W.P. mean?

PETER. Why do you want to know?

BOOTS. Because I want to know. Because
I think I've heard it before.

PETER. Oh.

BOOTS. Well?

PETER. I don't know.

BOOTS. What do you mean you don't know?

PETER. I mean,
I don't know.
I don't know what it means.
I made it up.

(*Beat.*

BOOTS *sits in the sand.*)

What's wrong?

(**PETER** *sits next to her.*

Pause.)

BOOTS. Why don't you ever tell me anything?

PETER. What are you talking about?

BOOTS. You never
You never
It's like I don't even know anything about you.

PETER. That's crazy.

BOOTS. But it's true.

PETER. What about the Twister mat? And the murals?

BOOTS. That stuff doesn't count.

PETER. Of course it does. It counts more than anything.

BOOTS. But it doesn't.

I don't *know* anything.

I don't *have* anything to *keep* from – from

(beat)

I didn't even know it was going to be your birthday.

(pause)

PETER. It was going to be my birthday.

BOOTS. I *know.*

Thanks for telling me.

(Beat.

PETER *stands.)*

PETER. Hey!

(He cups his hands over his eyes like a look out

even though it is dark.

He shines his flashlight across the water.)

Do you think we've *lost* them?

BOOTS. What?

PETER. Do you think we've lost them?

(beat)

The ones that are chasing us.

Everyone? And our families?

(beat)

BOOTS. I don't care.

PETER. Did you prepare the raft for – for
sailing?

(beat)

BOOTS. Sorry. I'm just
I'm not in the mood.

PETER. But this is what we do.
    Together. We tell stories.

BOOTS. *(sarcastically)* Why don't you tell me a story about
    your birthday?

PETER. About my birthday?

BOOTS. Yeah. Your birthday. Something real.

PETER. I

> *(He stops.*
>
> *Beat.)*

I don't have a story about my birthday.

> *(pause)*

BOOTS. I think I should go.

> *(She gets up.)*

PETER. Go where?

BOOTS. I don't know.
    I just want to leave this place.

PETER. But you can't go.

BOOTS. Of course, I can.

PETER. How?

BOOTS. I'll just walk
    that way.

PETER. But you'll just come back.

BOOTS. I won't.

PETER. You will because
    you keep ending up here
    even when you don't mean to.

BOOTS. That's not true.

PETER. You know it's true.
    You always touch your bangs like that when you lie.

BOOTS. So you're saying I can never leave, ever?
    Is that what you're saying?

PETER. No. What I'm saying is
    obviously there is something you're looking for.

Maybe when you find it
you can just
go.

(beat)

BOOTS. When I came here I was trying to remember the last thing you said to me.
Do you think that's it?

PETER. Maybe.

BOOTS. O.K.K.B.W.P. – was that it?

PETER. The last thing I said to you?

BOOTS. Yeah.

PETER. No.

BOOTS. Well, then what was it?

PETER. I'm sorry, I don't know.

BOOTS. Peter!

PETER. But I can help you remember.

(beat)

BOOTS. How?

PETER. Basically.
The only way to remember anything –

(Beat.

He tries to think of the best way to say it.)

Let me put it this way:
It's only when you stop thinking about the thing that you're
supposed to remember
that you remember it.

BOOTS. I don't know if that's right.

PETER. It's true.
It works for me all the time.
Try it.

*(**BOOTS** tries to think of something else.)*

BOOTS. How long do I have to do this for?

PETER. That's the thing.

You never know.

(beat)

Like one time,

I couldn't remember the name of the airplane

that dropped the bomb on Hiroshima.

For a whole day, I tried to remember, and I tried to remember,

and I tried to remember

but nothing.

Then, when I was walking home from school

I was looking at the ground and the shadow of a bird passed over

and just like that –

Enola Gay – and I remembered.

(beat)

BOOTS. It's not working.

PETER. It will eventually.

(beat)

Do you want to hear a story?

BOOTS. Is it real?

PETER. Why?

BOOTS. I only want to hear it if it's real this time.

PETER. Of course, it's real. It's what you asked for.

It's about my birthday.

BOOTS. Oh.

(beat)

PETER. I figured it would be something like –

Okay.

I would explain it to you like this:

The whole thing – it was a lovely party.

There were pink and red balloons and tiny animals molded out of chocolate ice cream and –

(Beat.

BOOTS *is listening attentively, but he gets lost anyway.)*

What am I saying?

The candles.

I was talking about the moment I blew out the candles.

BOOTS. *(confused)* The candles?

PETER. Um.

How else could I describe it to you?

(beat)

I blew out the candle.

I snapped my fingers, and backed into an empty space like this one.

(beat)

And in my mind – you were there.

Rubbing a red balloon over your hair so that the static made it stand up. And you were eating a melting rabbit – or was it an elephant? – and I saw you lick the ear or the trunk and I imagined you saying how lovely it was that the chocolate tasted like heaven.

You talked about heaven but you never asked me what I wished for when I blew out the flames.

(beat)

I pursed my lips like a whistle.

I closed my eyes and I was gone.

(beat)

I know you're not supposed to tell anybody those things that you think about when you breathe in to blow out the candles – but I just want you to know: my wish was to say it out loud.

(pause)

BOOTS. But your birthday is tomorrow.

PETER. Never mind.

BOOTS. No, no –

PETER. It was a dumb story.

BOOTS. It was a great story. I just

PETER. I know.

BOOTS. I just don't really understand.

I'm sorry.

(*Beat.*

They look at each other and then look away.)

Megan got her prom dress on Saturday.

PETER. Yeah?

(*beat*)

BOOTS. Favorites dance is on Friday.

PETER. Are you going?

BOOTS. I don't know.

It depends.

On who will be there.

PETER. Yeah.

Same.

(**BOOTS** *looks at him but doesn't say anything.*)

It'll probably be lame, so

BOOTS. But

PETER. What?

BOOTS. You can't go.

PETER. Of course, I can.

I can do whatever I want.

BOOTS. Okay.

PETER. You don't believe me.

That I could go

If I wanted to.

BOOTS. No, no.

I believe you.

PETER. I'll be there with my popsicle sticks
and you'll be wearing your crown.
Just like we imagined it.

BOOTS. *(sincerely)* Okay.

PETER. I know you don't believe it but it's true.
Wait for me there.
And we can
even figure out what happened that night.
We'll remember it all and we'll be so happy
you can't even know.

BOOTS. Are you asking me to the dance?

PETER. I mean, yes.
I mean, I guess so.

BOOTS. No one has ever asked me to a dance before.
What should I do?

PETER. Whatever you want!
But just be there.
Will you promise?

BOOTS. I promise.

(Beat.

Lights fade.)

Six

(The cafeteria.

A sea of tables.

Sounds of laughter and eating.

EGGS *stands alone holding a Styrofoam lunch tray.)*

EGGS. Today was a day of rain but no Boots.
I woke up at exactly 7:57 like always.
I knew the time but I thought it was Saturday
so I put on my baseball jersey and ran, like,
eight circles around my room before breakfast.
But then I remembered what day it was
and it wasn't Saturday.
I got back in bed and when I heard my mom pacing the hallway outside my room
I said very loudly through the door,
"My stomach hurts."
Nothing.
"My ear hurts," I said,
"I think it's infected."
Nothing.
"My stomach and my ears and my elbow feels ticklish right by the funny bone and
my arms are going numb."

"My everything hurts,"
I said,
louder this time.

At exactly 8:15 I was waiting for the bus.

Anyways.
My point is:
Boots was acting really weirs today.
Weird.

EGGS. *(cont.)* Gross.

Weirs.

New friends are hard to come by, I told her.

Not really, she said.

And she didn't sit next to me on the bus.

But then this thing happened. Between second and third period,

I saw her in the hallway

and she kind of looked at me and kind of smiled.

Like everything was okay again.

So, well. After that, I thought I would try to ask Boots to the Favorites Dance, again

at lunch when I saw her next.

Which was dumb, I guess.

But anyways, this is how it happened:

*(***EGGS** *navigates the sea of tables.*

They are pushed so close together

he can barely squeeze between them.

BOOTS *sits at a table far away,*

talking and laughing.)

It took me almost ten whole minutes to get to her in the lunchroom.

(He almost trips over unseen feet.)

Sorry! Sorry.

So, I carried my cold macaroni and cheese on my tray over to her table.

Her table with other girls like,

Ashley Tiggs who is so weirs, do you remember Ashley Tiggs?

Probably. Because she's so *weirs*.

Anyway. I had this open milk carton and it was spilling, kind of, because the tray was sliding in my hands.

But I walked right up to her,

and I was ready,

and I was like,

"Hi!"

(Awkward beat.

BOOTS *turns to him.)*

BOOTS. Oh. Hey.

(Long beat.

BOOTS *starts to turn back to her table.)*

EGGS. "I have a joke, do you want to hear it?"

My milk was almost gone, it was a puddle that became an ocean on my tray.

My macaroni was soggy in a Styrofoam pool, the tray was jumping out of my hands

and squeaking.

What was I going to say? I couldn't remember what I was going to say.

I just kept looking at Boots's thin bangs and how it looked like the tips kept getting longer while I was trying to remember,

so that by the time I even said anything, they brushed her eyelashes when she blinked and said:

BOOTS. Sure?

EGGS. "What did the waves – I mean,

what did the ocean say to the shore?"

I said finally, and I think my voice must have done something weird

when I said it because Ashley laughed

really loud right then.

She had cheese from the macaroni on her lips.

And I just watched Boots's eyelashes

when she looked right through me.

(beat)

And right then,
I wished my lunch wasn't floating away on my tray,
and I wondered where the time went.

(**BOOTS** *tries not to laugh.*)

BOOTS. I don't know.
I don't know.

(Long pause while she waits for the punch line.
Finally, **BOOTS** *laughs and turns back to her table.*
EGGS *speaks to his tray.)*

EGGS. "Wave,"
was what I managed to say after about a million years.

(**BOOTS** *exits talking and laughing with her friends.)*

"Nothing," I said,
"It just waved."

Seven

(Ragtime music.

BOOTS *walks back and forth*

like on a tightrope.

She blows a kiss.)

BOOTS. Heel, toe.

Heel, toe.

(She curtsies even though she is not wearing a skirt.

She looks up.)

Peter?

Don't come in here.

I'm getting ready.

I'm getting ready for Favorites Dance.

Just wait downstairs with Mom, Dad and Megan.

I'll only be a few hours!

*(***BOOTS*** *laughs.*

She stops.

Then she has an idea:)

Peter!

I have a story for you.

We're not going to Favorites Dance,

we're going to prom, remember?

(She closes her eyes.)

High school.

Junior year.

But the main thing is – I walk into the gym

all decorated with streamers and balloons,

and I see you swaying in the middle of the dance floor.

*(***BOOTS*** *sways slowly by herself,*

her eyes still closed.)

BOOTS. *(cont.)* Billie Holiday is playing.

The slow one that we like.

(Lights begin to dim.

No music.)

I can see you

behind Ashley Tiggs and her weirs boyfriend, David Grover.

I can see your face over David's shoulder where Ashley's pink chin is resting.

They move steady.

And so do you because it's your favorite song.

You're all alone, dancing with your eyes closed.

Everything is –

soft, like David's shoulder pads, his suit jacket exactly one size too small.

And you sway, softly, just like this.

(She sways alone with her eyes closed.)

I tuck my hair behind my ears

and just like that –

I slip right through Ashley.

And David,

and the whole softly swaying crowd like a breeze or a whisper on hot breath.

One more step and I am standing in front of you, floating.

One more step

and everything disappears, but not really.

They – Ashley, David, the gym and everybody in it –

they just keep moving back and back from my eyes like the tide.

And I don't say a word

but curtsey.

As you tip your hat

that's really a crown.

BOOTS. *(cont.)* You say, May I have this dance?

And I say, I suppose.

As I take your hand and the music changes.

And when our fingers touch they are different from *their* fingers.

Because when we hold hands, it is different from the way everyone else holds hands.

When our necks and palms rest together they don't sweat.

And when the music plays only we can hear it

as we don't dance, but sway, like the sea.

But when I open my eyes -

you're gone.

So, I look for you.

I search the gym floor, the parking lots and empty spaces.

Long, long hallways, swinging lockers, open and cringing,

the links of the metal grates that block the math wing, under the florescent lights,

the reflection of the display case,

the dust on the trophies,

the grooves of the linoleum tile.

I'm flying trying to find you.

But I'm running in place.

And I'm dancing

all alone.

Eight

(The lights are dim with impressions of

a slow moving disco ball.

Billie Jean *plays.**

EGGS *crosses and uncrosses his arms by the bleachers.*

His shoelaces are tied together.

He speaks to unseen people at the dance.)

EGGS. I hate this song.

I can't dance to this song.

If I could leave my body, then I could dance, I guess.

I just don't have any rhythm.

I just don't know where to put my feet.

That's why. Sorry. Or. I'm waiting for someone, I mean. But thanks.

I'm just saving the dance is all. Thanks. Don't go –

Hey! Did you know that five out of three people have trouble with fractions?

(He tries to take a step forward.

He trips over his feet.

Laughter.)

Thanks, thank you. I, uh, it's my shoes. They're tied together and they won't come undone.

Hey, what's the difference between a fish and a piano?

Sorry.

Yeah, that was lame. Sorry.

(He is bumped from behind.

He trips again.

Laughter.)

Alright, alright. I mean, sorry.

---

*See Music Use Note on page 3.

(**BOOTS** *enters.*

BOOTS *is wearing Megan's prom dress. She is woefully overdressed for the Favorites Dance.*

She moves through the unseen dancers uneasily.

Everyone is looking at her.

She spots **EGGS**.

She approaches him and stands next to him by the bleachers.

He doesn't acknowledge her.

She speaks above the music.)

BOOTS. Hi.

(*beat*)

I'm wearing Megan's prom dress.
She doesn't know.

(*beat*)

Your shoelaces are tied together.

EGGS. I know.

(*beat*)

Why are you dressed like that?
You look weird.

BOOTS. I said its Megan's.

(*beat*)

These things should be more –
formal, you know what I mean?

(**EGGS** *doesn't respond.*

BOOTS *looks through the crowd expectantly.)*

EGGS. What are you doing?

BOOTS. I'm waiting for someone.

EGGS. Oh.

(*beat*)

So am I.

(long pause)

BOOTS. Do you want me to help you with that?

EGGS. What?

BOOTS. Your shoes.

Do you want me to help you untie your shoes?

EGGS. No.

(beat)

I did it on purpose.

BOOTS. Oh.

EGGS. Could you not stand here, please?
People are looking at me weird
because you're standing here.

BOOTS. Why?

EGGS. Because you look ridiculous.

(beat)

BOOTS. Fine.

(She walks to the other end of the dance floor.

The disco ball moves slower.

A slow dance.

Billie Holiday's, I'll Be Seeing You*, *plays.*

BOOTS *looks excited.*

She searches the crowd expectantly.

A few moments pass.

EGGS *watches her across the room.*

He speaks to himself.)

EGGS. Oh. Hey, Boots.
Hey, Boots that's a cool dress.
Hey! Boots. I was waiting,
looking
I was looking for you.

---

*See Music Use Note on page 3.

EGGS. *(cont.)* Boots.

I was wondering if maybe you wanted to dance.

*(**EGGS** makes a decision.*

He takes a step forward.

He trips and falls.

Laughter.

He picks himself up.

More laughter.

He shuffles out of the gym, embarrassed.)

Nine

(Outside the gym.

Music from inside the dance can be heard.

EGGS *sits on the floor in front of his locker,*

struggling with his shoelaces.

PETER *sits on top of* **EGGS** *' locker,*

letting his legs dangle.

EGGS *doesn't see him.)*

EGGS. Stupid

shoes.

Stupid

dance.

I hate everybody.

(He looks in the direction of the gym.)

You and you and you and

you.

I hate you.

(beat)

You were supposed to be here.

(The laces on his shoes won't untangle.

EGGS *gives up and buries his head in his hands.*

Long, long pause.

PETER *climbs down from the locker.*

He sits in front of **EGGS**.

He begins to untie his shoelaces.

EGGS *doesn't look up.*

He speaks from inside of his elbows.)

EGGS. Do you remember me?

PETER. Of course.

Why do you think I would forget?

EGGS. I don't know.

> *(beat)*

> What are you doing?

PETER. Leaving.

> You're right.

> This dance is lame.

EGGS. Tell me about it.

PETER. And you're right,

> Ashley Tiggs is so weirs.

EGGS. Thank you.

> I feel like I'm the only one that notices that.

PETER. I know.

> *(beat)*

> You know what I was just thinking about?

EGGS. What?

PETER. That awesome baseball card collection you have.

> *(**EGGS** brightens a little at the thought.)*

EGGS. Oh, yeah.

> I guess it's a pretty good one.

PETER. Pretty good?

> It's epic.

> I bet those kids in there would freak out if they knew
> how awesome it was.

EGGS. I don't know about that.

PETER. Why not?

EGGS. I don't know. I just think –

> I just think that they think baseball cards are for kids
> or something.

> I bet they would think it was really dumb.

PETER. What? That's crazy.

EGGS. Not really.

PETER. That's so stupid, you know?

> Who even cares about these guys?

EGGS. I know.

PETER. It's like they don't know *anything*.

EGGS. I *know*.

PETER. You'll probably like,

make a million dollars off that collection

by the time you're in high school –

then they'll appreciate how awesome it is.

EGGS. I *know!*

(*long pause*)

PETER. You shouldn't have to put up with this.

You know what you should do?

EGGS. Go back in there and tell them I'll be a millionaire in four years?

PETER. No.

I think you should leave.

EGGS. Leave?

PETER. Yeah, just get out of here.

Go home, put on some music, and sort through your baseball cards.

Why waste time being miserable, when you could be doing something that actually makes you happy?

EGGS. Yeah.

PETER. I mean, like,

what would you even be missing?

Like, crappy music? Sweaty hands?

EGGS. Weirsss…

PETER. I know! I wished I had left every dance I had ever been to!

EGGS. Me too!

PETER. Well, now is your chance.

(**PETER** *opens* **EGGS**'s *locker.*

He takes out **EGGS**'s *bag and hands it to him.*)

Here you are:

You ticket to freedom.

*(**EGGS** laughs and takes it.)*

EGGS. Thanks.

(He starts walking down the hallway, but stops looking off into the gym.)

EGGS. Hey, I was just thinking.

If you stay,

we can headbang by the bleachers.

PETER. I can't stay.

(beat)

EGGS. Yeah. I was just kidding.

I – nevermind.

PETER. What?

EGGS. Nothing. It's stupid.

PETER. No, what were you going to say?

EGGS. It's just –

(beat)

What's the last thing that happens?

(long beat)

PETER. I sit on my bed for a long, long time.

(beat)

EGGS. What do you think about?

PETER. I think about how I woke up late this morning

but how it was okay because the bus came late too.

I think about those seven extra minutes of sleep.

I think about how the paint of the four square court by the playground is chipping and how all the basketballs are deflated and won't bounce.

But then I think about how you can't see any of those things from an airplane.

I think about the moment before I know the teacher is going to call on me

and how I look down at my worksheet just in time,

pretending I wasn't thinking about something else the whole time.

EGGS. That's all?

Is that all you think about?

PETER. I think about how the texture on my ceiling looks like bear claws.

And – I don't know why -

but I started crying and then I got angry that I was crying

and I felt stupid

like someone was watching and I was crying to impress them.

EGGS. Do you think about me?

PETER. No.

EGGS. Do you think about Boots?

PETER. No.

(beat)

I just think about everything that makes me mad like even, it sounds dumb,

but when the wind knocks your hat off,

or how teachers think you're stupid

or when you say something you didn't mean to say.

And after a while it wasn't even specific.

It was like my whole body was focused on just being mad.

And then for like one second I felt like I could do anything.

(beat)

EGGS. Was I a bad friend?

PETER. You're my best friend.

(long pause)

EGGS. Do you think –

if I changed my mind, which I haven't,

but if I did – if I stayed should I ask Boots to dance?
Or would that be weird?

PETER. Be funnier.

Girls will like you.

EGGS. I'm *trying.*

PETER. She has seen you naked, though.

EGGS. I knew you'd say that.

(They look at each other.

EGGS *takes off his bag.*

He hands it to **PETER.***)*

EGGS. I just – I'm sorry.

There's something I have to do.

*(***EGGS** *runs into the gym.*

Lights fade on **PETER** *holding the bag.)*

Ten

*(***BOOTS*** *waits expectantly.*

A slow dance is playing, Billie Holiday's Keeps On Rainin'.*

EGGS *enters.*

He stands alone, awkwardly,

on the other end of the dance floor.

The song plays – ***EGGS*** *waits.*

He watches ***BOOTS***.

She turns and looks at him.

After a moment they walk toward each other.

The song plays.

EGGS *holds out his hand for a dance.*

BOOTS *takes his hand.*

They figure out how to slow dance.

As the song continues to play, they move closer and closer until they embrace, holding each other in a hug.

Lights fade.)

---

* See Music Use Note on page 3

Eleven

(A significant shift: though we are back in the tree house, everything should feel different.

This is the last time **BOOTS** *saw* **PETER**.

A night without stars.

There is a chill in the air.

BOOTS, *for the first time, is not wearing boots.*

She wears pajamas and a hoodie.

She waits.

PETER *comes up the rope ladder, out of breath.)*

PETER. Sorry.

BOOTS. Peter.

PETER. The whole way here I was thinking of something funny to tell you like,

I flushed my watch down the toilet!

or

I thought you said *ten* thirty!

or

Time flies! Or something.

But then I realized none of it was that funny.

*(***BOOTS*** just looks at him.*

PETER *looks away, slightly embarrassed,*

and then turns back to see her feet for the first time.)

You're not wearing your rain boots. I thought you were the type of girl who always

wears rain boots even when it's not raining.

BOOTS. I thought I'd give them a rest.

I thought I'd try something different.

PETER. It's kind of weird.

Boots without her boots.

BOOTS. Did you bring your flashlight?

PETER. This is it.

We're alone in the tree house.

BOOTS. We're alone.

PETER. What happens now?

(Beat.

They look at each other.)

BOOTS. It's a surprise.

PETER. Should we tell stories?

BOOTS. No,

we're too old for stories.

Tonight, we'll try something new.

PETER. Like what?

(pause)

BOOTS. We

sit very quietly and listen for owls.

PETER. Is that the surprise?

BOOTS. Shh!

Just listen.

(They look at each other

until they are too embarrassed to look at each other.

They listen for owls.)

PETER. I don't hear anything.

BOOTS. Just listen!

(They listen.

BOOTS *moves a little closer.)*

You can take my hand if you want.

(She holds out her hand.

PETER *doesn't take it.)*

– to *wave* to the owls.

(She holds her wrist with her other hand and

waves to the owls. A cover-up.)

BOOTS. *(cont.)* Hellooo, owls!

PETER. Shhh.

BOOTS. *(whispering)* Everything is so quiet.

> *(Long pause.*
>
> *(She moves a little closer.)*

The owls are holding their breath.

> (**PETER** *points his flashlight.)*

PETER. Can you scoot back a little bit?
All I can hear is your breathing.

BOOTS. Oh.
Sorry.

> (**BOOTS** *moves away.*
>
> *Beat.)*

PETER. I see one.
But he's not making any sound.

BOOTS. Where?

> (**PETER** *points his flashlight.)*

PETER. There. In the leaves.

BOOTS. Your light is reflecting.

PETER. Do you think it hurts his eyes?

BOOTS. Probably.

PETER. He's not even blinking.

BOOTS. You're probably blinding him.

PETER. He looks dead.

BOOTS. He's not dead.

PETER. Maybe owls don't blink.

BOOTS. Put your light down.

PETER. I'm trying to see.

BOOTS. I think you've seen him.
What are you doing?

> (**PETER** *holds his flashlight steady.)*

BOOTS. Peter.

> *(silence)*

> Peter.

> *(beat)*

> *Pete –*

> Er.

> *Peter.*

> Peter, put your light down.

> *Peter put your light down.*

> Peter –

PETER. He blinked.

> *(**PETER** shuts his flashlight off.*

> *Beat.)*

BOOTS. You turned your light off.

PETER. It was hurting my eyes.

BOOTS. Hey, Peter?

PETER. What?

BOOTS. I don't remember.

> *(Silence.*

> *In the glow of **BOOTS**' flashlight,*

> *we can see her looking at **PETER** in the dark.)*

PETER. I should probably go now.

> *(**PETER** stands.)*

BOOTS. We can tell stories if you want.

> We're not too old.

> I like stories.

PETER. I'm too tired.

BOOTS. But you said

PETER. I know. I guess I just don't know any.

> Sorry.

BOOTS. And your surprise.

> I still have a surprise for you.

PETER. What is it?

BOOTS. I can't just say.

    I have to

    surprise you with it.

PETER. Okay.

BOOTS. But before that.

    I can tell a story.

PETER. What kind of story is it?

BOOTS. A good one.

    Obviously.

PETER. Is it scary?

    (**BOOTS** *considers*)

BOOTS. It's very scary.

    So scary, actually, that I get scared,

    even when I'm the one telling it.

    You'll probably have to put your arm around me

    so I'm not too afraid.

    (beat)

    Just kidding.

PETER. Did you make it up just now?

    I don't want to hear it,

    if you made it up just now.

BOOTS. No.

    No, of course not.

    I

    heard it somewhere.

    It's an old story.

PETER. I don't believe you.

    You always touch your bangs like that when you lie.

BOOTS. Peter, how old are you?

PETER. Almost thirteen.

BOOTS. Just checking.

Do you want to hear this story or not?

(silence)

Peter?

(beat)

I was just kidding you.
Are you okay?

(beat)

You're acting like you don't even want to be here.
I thought we said at your locker today
I thought we said we'd stay out all night in the tree house.
I thought

PETER. I know.

I just
changed my mind, I guess.
I'm just tired.
I thought it would be fun,
but I was wrong.

(long beat)

BOOTS. *(hurt)* Well.

Are you going to leave then?

PETER. I'm sorry.

BOOTS. What?

(beat)

PETER. I'm sorry for acting like a jerk all the time.

BOOTS. You don't act like a jerk all the time.

PETER. No, I do.

And I'm sorry.

BOOTS. Okay?

(beat)

PETER. I have a story.

BOOTS. *(teasing)* Did you make it up just now?

Because I don't want to hear it if you made it up just now.

PETER. *(serious)* No.

It's an old story.

BOOTS. Cool.

PETER. It's the story of how we met.

BOOTS. I love that story!

Can I tell it?

PETER. No, I want to tell it.

I want to tell it different this time.

BOOTS. Okay.

PETER. This story starts about a million years ago –

BOOTS. Two.

(beat)

It was two years ago.

Sorry.

Continue.

PETER. It takes place after Mr. Martin's fourth period gym class.

BOOTS. I hated him!

PETER. Outside,

just after everyone had finished playing kick ball.

And the new kid,

it was his first day at school, by the way,

he was carrying the ball back inside.

*(**BOOTS** starts laughing,*

anticipating the next parts of the story.)

And this girl,

in these big, yellow rain boots,

just runs up

and *kicks*

the kick ball right out of the new kids' hands.

BOOTS. It was so funny!

The look on your face!

Then you were all like,

What's the deal?

And I was like,

Nice to meet you!

(She laughs.)

PETER. No, no.

That's not how it happened.

BOOTS. Pretty much.

That was the day I showed you the tree house.

Remember?

PETER. But that's not how this story goes.

Remember?

This is different.

BOOTS. Then what happens?

PETER. The girl kicks the ball right out of his hands

and it sails way, way

out over the soccer fields.

And the boy keeps walking

just like nothing ever happened.

(beat)

BOOTS. But she stops him.

And she says,

My name is Cate,

but pretty much everyone calls me Boots.

PETER. No, that's the thing.

She doesn't. The girls kicks the ball right out of his hands,

and she runs back to her friends

because she has a lot of other friends

who are really awesome and great and nice to her.

PETER. *(cont.)* She runs back to her friends.

    Like nothing ever happened.

BOOTS. But that's not what happened.

    I would never do that, that's mean.

PETER. No, not mean.

    The boy doesn't get upset or anything.

    He doesn't laugh it off and follow her inside.

    He doesn't chase her yellow rain boots and try to get her back.

    He doesn't walk to the tree house with her after school.

    In that moment,

    he just

    keeps walking.

BOOTS. But then

    he comes back.

    Because that's how they meet.

PETER. In this story,

    he just keeps walking.

BOOTS. If you want,

    it can be that

    the boy

    kicks the ball right out of the girl's hands

    and she's like,

    Hey –

PETER. No.

    He just

    keeps

    walking.

BOOTS. Well, where does he go?

    Who does he talk to?

    Does he go to the tree house?

PETER. He walks into the soccer fields.

    He makes a chain of dandelions.

    He plucks grass.

    And he doesn't talk to anybody.

BOOTS. And then the girl follows him
Because she would never leave him.

PETER. She doesn't follow him
She forgets it ever happened.
She goes back to her friends.
She laughs.
And at the end of the day,
her boots make a crunching sound as she runs all the way home.

BOOTS. But that's not how it happened.

PETER. No.

BOOTS. Then how does it end?
If the boy and the girl never meet,
how does the story end?

PETER. The girl's story,
the girl outgrows her yellow rain boots.
But the boy,
his story ends tonight.

(long pause)

BOOTS. You didn't have to come if you were going to be like this.
If you don't like me like that,
you can just say it.

PETER. I came here tonight to tell you,
I'm going away
to a place where you can't go.

(beat)

I came here tonight to tell you,
I'm sorry.

*(**BOOTS** and **PETER** look at each other for a long time.*
They aren't too embarrassed to look each other in the eyes.
Time passes.)

BOOTS. So, this is the end.

PETER. This is the end.

BOOTS. Why can't I come?

PETER. You don't understand.

> This time,
>
> if you understood,
>
> you would know why I have to do this by myself.

> *(long pause)*

BOOTS. I have a story.

> The old one,
>
> a real story, from a book I read.
>
> An old story about a woman in a long dress and a man in a top hat.
>
> They ride in carriages.
>
> And after it is too late at night to be riding in carriages,
>
> and the man walks the woman to his door,
>
> the woman asks a question in letters:
>
> O.K.K.B.W.P.

PETER. O.K.K. – ?

BOOTS. Yeah. O.K.K.B.W.P.

PETER. What does that mean?

BOOTS. One Kind Kiss Before We Part?

PETER. I'm sorry.

BOOTS. No, it was a dumb story.

PETER. No, it's – no.

> I just –

BOOTS. No, I shouldn't have said anything, I'm sorry.

PETER. No.

> *(beat)*

> I'm just – really sorry.
>
> But there
>
> I have somewhere I have to be.

(**PETER** *exits.*

BOOTS *does not follow.*)

End of play.